Cool Rules

by Bobbi Weiss and Suzanne Weyn

Illustrated by Mark Marderosian

Cover illustrated by Barry Goldberg

SCHOLASTIC INC.

New York Toronto London Auckland Sydney
Mexico City New Delhi Hong Kong Buenos Aires

Published by Scholastic Inc.,
90 Old Sherman Turnpike, Danbury, Connecticut 06816.

ISBN 0-439-56305-4

First Scholastic Printing, June 2004

Chapters

Chapter 1
Who's Cool?

"Yes . . . Yes . . . Got it!" Jimmy Neutron exclaimed as he watched a fly buzzing down the school hallway. Then he began to furiously scribble notes and diagrams on a pad.

"What are you doing, Jimmy?" Carl Wheezer asked his friend.

"I'm computing the velocity of a fly circling the school and multiplying it by the square root of the speed of light in order to calibrate this new jet pack. I want to get to the lunch room before all the Purple Flurp is gone," Jimmy explained.

“Wow, Jimmy,” Carl said admiringly. “Have you ever computed the velocity of a llama?”

Just then Cindy Vortex and Libby walked up. “Hey, Nerdtron, could you move out of the way?” Cindy snapped. “Your hair is blocking my view!”

Carl jumped to his friend's defense. "Jimmy's very busy calculating the speed of Purple Flurp," he began.

"Who cares about some geeky experiment?" Libby interrupted. "We're trying to see Nick's new jacket."

Jimmy and Carl watched as all the kids crowded around Nick, the coolest kid in school.

"Big deal. I don't get it," Jimmy muttered. "What's so great about a jacket?"

"It's not just *any* jacket," Carl explained. "It's Nick's jacket, and everything Nick has is cool because Nick is cool. No one is cooler than Nick."

Their friend Sheen joined them. "Ultra Lord is cooler than Nick," he said. "But if you don't count Ultra Lord, then, yeah, Nick is the coolest."

"I could be cooler than Nick if I wanted to be!" Jimmy said.

Carl and Sheen didn't answer. That was because they were laughing too hard to speak. "No offense, Jimmy, but I don't think so," Carl said when he caught his breath.

"I can be cool!" Jimmy told them. "You'll see."

Chapter 2
The Cool Factor

After school, Jimmy went straight to his lab. “I just know I could be as cool as Nick,” he said to his robot dog, Goddard. “What do you think makes a person cool?”

Goddard beeped and his eyes flashed. Words appeared on his digital readout: PEOPLE ADMIRE THEM.

"True," said Jimmy. "But there must be more to it. Let's see . . . " Jimmy went to his computer and downloaded data about people who were cool. He compiled lists of sports

stars, recording stars, and TV and movie celebrities. “Now, how can I be as cool as they are?” Jimmy wondered. “Goddard, perform analysis of the cool factor.”

Gears whirred and lights flashed. Finally, an answer appeared on Goddard's display.

"That's it!" Jimmy exclaimed. "Next stop, Coolsville. Population: me!"

Chapter 3
Growth Spurt

The next morning, Jimmy's friends were waiting for him outside of their classroom. "Say," said Sheen, "did you, like, have a growth spurt or something?"

"You definitely look bigger," Carl added.

Jimmy grinned at his friends. "Gentlemen, you haven't seen anything yet." He tapped the hydraulic controls on either side of his new Extenso-Legs and—with a mechanical *SHOOF!*—he grew to seven feet tall!

“You’re looking at Jimmy Neutron, the soon-to-be coolest kid on the basketball court!”

Jimmy headed into the gym—but he was so tall that his forehead bumped the top of the doorway! As he staggered backward, his Extenso-Legs buckled under him. Then came a flash as the mechanism short-circuited and shot him up into the air like a rocket!

"Hey, that *IS* pretty cool!" Sheen exclaimed as Jimmy sailed past him.

Chapter 4
Dance-atronic Belt

The next day, Jimmy was ready with a new tactic. "Looking cool and having cool moves is what really matters," he told Goddard. "Watch this!" He pushed a button, and his auto-valet whirled around him.

Jimmy emerged with a cool new look. “The kids will think I’ve really got it going on now,” he said as he headed out of the lab. Suddenly he stopped. His baggy pants were slipping. “I almost forgot the dance-atronic belt I invented,” he said, running

back to get it. “Not only will it hold up my extrabaggy pants, but it also will give me the moves I need to be cool.”

When Jimmy got to school, he set his belt on "strut."

"Hey, look at Neutron!" Cindy said to Libby. "Something about the way he's walking seems almost . . . cool."

Jimmy heard her and smiled. "Just wait until you see me bust a move," he said.

Jimmy hit a button on the dance-atronic belt. Dance music blared from its special embedded microcircuits. With the push of another button, Jimmy began to perform all the latest dance moves. A crowd of kids gathered to watch him.

The lights on Jimmy's belt glowed brighter and brighter the faster Jimmy

danced. They flashed and changed color. Jimmy flipped in the air. He spun on the floor.

He twirled and kicked. But just as he was getting ready to execute his most impressive move, the dance-atronic belt burst apart, flying through the air!

Without the belt, Jimmy's big baggy pants fell down!

"Err, I'm still working out a few bugs," he muttered as he stumbled away, clutching his pants.

Chapter 5
The Admirator Ray

Jimmy went home that afternoon and thought hard. He remembered what Goddard had told him. Cool people were admired. "Brain blast! Why didn't I think of that before?" Jimmy cried.

After dinner that night, Jimmy put the finishing touches on his new invention. "Behold the Admirator Ray!" he said to Goddard. "One zap will polarize my body chemistry, increasing my personal magnetism a hundred times over. It's going to be a Neutron admire-athon!"

At breakfast the next morning, Jimmy's mother had a strange look in her eyes. "Do you really have to go to school?" she asked pleadingly. "You're so wonderful that I can't stand for you to leave."

His dad smiled fondly at Jimmy. "Jimmy is beyond wonderful. He's wonderiffic!"

"But am I cool?" Jimmy asked.

"The coolest!" his parents shouted together.

Chapter 6
Jimmy Cooltron

When Jimmy got to school, everyone who saw him was awed.

"Neutron, you are the coolest!" Cindy gushed. "Would you sign my autograph book?"

"Mine, too!" added Libby.

The ray was definitely working!

Even Carl and Sheen were dazzled. "I can't believe I'm going to say this, but he's as cool as Ultra Lord," Sheen said.

Jimmy just smiled. "Being cool is child's play for your average genius," he thought to himself.

In class, Miss Fowl asked Jimmy to stand at the front of the room. "Do you want me to solve a math problem or something?" Jimmy asked.

"No," Miss Fowl answered. "Just stand there so we can admire you!"

The whole class gazed at Jimmy. “Neutron,” said Nick in a voice filled with admiration, “you are so . . . so . . . ” He searched for the word. “*Cool!*” he finally blurted.

A crowd began to form outside the classroom. Then a flood of students swept into the room and surrounded Jimmy. "Sign my hand, Jimmy," a girl requested.

“Will you be my best friend?” asked a boy.

“Can I have a little piece of your hair?” another girl asked.

Being admired by everyone was beginning to make Jimmy a little nervous.

Jimmy squeezed out of the overcrowded classroom and into the hall. “Calm down,” he told everyone. “I’m not really that cool. All I did was create an Admirator Ray . . . ” But the kids were chanting Jimmy’s name so loudly that no one heard him.

“That ray must have been too strong,” Jimmy realized as the crowd pushed in on him. “I need to get back to my lab and fix this!” Jimmy took a deep breath, then pushed his way through the throng and ran as fast as he could!

Chapter 7
Cool No More

The admiring kids chased Jimmy down the hall, out the doors of the school, and down the street. Everyone who saw Jimmy joined in the chase. Soon the entire town was running after him in a frenzy of admiration.

Finally, Jimmy reached his house. His parents had built a statue of him on the front lawn. "Jimmy's home!" they cried happily when they spotted him.

Jimmy ran past them, straight to his lab, and locked the doors behind him. “I sure hope this works,” he murmured as he positioned himself before the Admirator Ray and hit the REVERSE switch.

A few moments later, Jimmy went back outside and faced the crowd. At first no one said anything.

Cindy was the first to speak. "What are we all doing here at the dork's house?"

Jimmy's mom spoke up next. "James Isaac Neutron, why aren't you at school?" she scolded. "And who are all these people?"

Jimmy tried to explain. "Well, you see, they thought I was cool and—"

“Cool?” Cindy interrupted. “You? I think you’re even nerdier than you were yesterday.”

Everyone turned and walked away, shaking their heads.

"Don't worry, Jimmy," Carl said. "You may not be cool anymore, but we still like you."

"And Ultra Lord likes you," added Sheen.

"Thanks, you guys," Jimmy said with a smile, as Goddard licked his hand. He knew

his friends would always stand by him whether he was cool or not—and that was really cool.